For Maurice Gilmour –c.m.

First published in Great Britain by Andersen Press Ltd., 2004
Printed and bound in Italy by Grafiche AZ, Verona
First American edition, 2005
1 3 5 7 9 10 8 6 4 2

www.fsgkidsbooks.com

Library of Congress Control Number: 2004105656

Once Upon an Ordinary School Day

Story by Colin McNaughton
Pictures by Satoshi Kitamura

Farrar Straus Giroux
New York

Once upon an ordinary school day,
an ordinary boy woke from his ordinary dreams,
got out of his ordinary bed, had an ordinary pee and
an ordinary bath, put on his ordinary clothes,
and ate his ordinary breakfast.
  The ordinary boy brushed his ordinary teeth,
kissed his ordinary mom goodbye, and set off
for his ordinary school.

And as he walked along the ordinary sidewalks,
past the ordinary shops, and across the ordinary streets,

the ordinary boy thought his ordinary thoughts.

And when he reached the ordinary school, the ordinary boy had an ordinary game of soccer with his ordinary friends until the ordinary school bell rang.

The ordinary boy went into his ordinary
classroom and sat at his ordinary desk.
Then something quite out of the
ordinary happened . . .

"Good morning, everybody!"
said a quite extraordinary figure
bounding into the classroom.
"My name is Mr. Gee,
and I'm your new teacher.
Now, you don't know me and
I don't know you,
so, to help me *get* to know you,
I've had an idea . . ."

As Mr. Gee handed out paper,
he said, "For our first lesson together
I want you to listen to some music and
I want you to let the music make
pictures in your heads.
Is that clear?"

And the ordinary children whispered, "He's bonkers!"
"He's as nutty as a fruitcake!" "Music?" "Pictures?"
"What's he talking about?" And Mr. Gee said, "Shush, just
close your eyes, open your ears, and listen."

And the music began:
a rumbling, rolling,
thunderous music
that boomed and
crashed around
the classroom.

Suddenly it stopped. And Mr. Gee said,
"Tell me what the music made you think of."
One girl shouted, "Stampeding horses!"
Someone else said, "No, it was cars!"
And the ordinary boy said, "I saw elephants,
and there were hundreds of them!"

"Yes," said Mr. Gee, laughing. "Isn't it wonderful?
Now I want all of you to try to put
what you hear on paper.
Start writing!"

    And as the music
grew and swooped and
danced and dived once more,
the ordinary boy began to write.
He used words he didn't fully understand
and his story made no sense but it didn't matter
and he didn't care. And he wrote as fast as he could
but it would never be fast enough—there was too
much to say. It was as if a dam had burst in his head
and words just came flooding out . . .

. . . and the words were his toys and he was lost,
lost in the game—the storytelling game.
    And it was *extraordinary* . . .

And the other children?
Some wrote stories about giants
and some about magic. Some wrote of brave girls
and some of boys with lightning-shaped scars
on their foreheads.
   Some just made stuff up because
the music didn't mean anything to them,
and Pauline Crawford read *Wonder Woman*.

Some wrote stories
they thought would please
the teacher and some became
heroes and some became villains
and some thought the whole thing
was silly and Billy Pearson fell asleep—
"Perchance to dream,"
said Mr. Gee.

And at the end of that extraordinary school day,
the ordinary boy saw Mr. Gee getting into his car.
"Sir," said the ordinary boy, "that was the best lesson ever.
I've never felt like that before. It was magic!"
"Still think I'm bonkers?" said Mr. Gee, smiling.
The ordinary boy blushed.
"I can't wait to read your story tonight,"
said Mr. Gee. "See you tomorrow."
And he disappeared in a cloud of smoke
out of the school gates.

And when it was bedtime,
the ordinary boy put on his ordinary
pajamas, brushed his ordinary teeth,
had his ordinary pee, kissed his
ordinary mom and dad, and went
to sleep in his ordinary bed . . .

. . . and had
extraordinary
dreams.